CHARRO CLAUS
and the Tejas Kid

written and illustrated by
XAVIER GARZA

IT'S THE NIGHT BEFORE CHRISTMAS and a boy named Vincent is getting ready for bed. He is spending Christmas Eve with his Tío Pancho on their old family farm near the Texas / Mexico border.

✣

ES NOCHEBUENA y un niño llamado Vicente se prepara para ir a la cama. Pasará la Navidad con su Tío Pancho en su viejo rancho familiar cerca de la frontera de Tejas con México.

HE'S TIRED FROM MILKING the cows and feeding the chickens. But as soon as he shuts his eyes, he hears footsteps up on the roof.

Thump, thump, thump!

"Who's up there?" he hears his Tío Pancho yelling. Vincent looks out the window. His uncle is climbing up a ladder. Vincent puts on his boots and runs outside. Quietly...quietly, he follows his uncle up the ladder.

ESTÁ CANSADO DE ORDEÑAR las vacas y alimentar a las gallinas. Pero en cuanto cierra los ojos escucha pasos en el techo.

¡Tump, tump, tump!

—¿Quién está ahí arriba? —escucha que grita su Tío Pancho. Vicente se asoma por la ventana. Su tío sube por una escalera. Vicente se pone las botas y corre afuera. Calladito...calladito, sigue a su tío por la escalera.

"Aiiiii!" Vincent has to cover his mouth to keep from screaming. His uncle is on the roof talking to...Santa Claus!

"Cousin Santa Claus!" Tío Pancho cries. They give each other a big abrazo.

Vincent is stunned. My uncle Pancho and Santa Claus are cousins?

"I need your help, *primo*," says Santa Claus. "The border along the Rio Grande is too long for an old man like me. Especially when I need to deliver presents to every single corner of the world. Can you help me?"

✦

—¡AYYYYYYY!— Vicente se tapa la boca para no gritar. Su tío está en el techo platicando con...¡Santa Claus!

—¡Primo Santa Claus! —exclama su Tío Pancho. Y se dan un gran abrazo.

Vicente está sorprendido. ¿Mi Tío Pancho y Santa Claus son primos?

—Necesito tu ayuda, primo —dice Santa Claus—. La frontera del Río Grande es muy grande para un viejo como yo. Especialmente si necesito entregar regalos en cada esquina del mundo. ¿Me puedes ayudar?

TÍO PANCHO FROWNS. "Would I have to wear a red and white suit?"

"Not even," answers Santa. "You can wear that mariachi outfit you wore back in your singing days."

"But I was a lot younger then—and thinner too!"

"Never mind that," says Santa Claus. He grabs Tío Pancho's hand, and—in the blink of an eye—they slip down the chimney together like magic.

EL TÍO PANCHO FRUNCE EL CEÑO. —¿Y tendré que ponerme un traje rojo y blanco?

—Ni eso —responde Santa—. Puedes ponerte ese traje de mariachi que usabas en aquella época en que cantabas.

—Pero yo era más joven entonces. ¡Y también más flaco!

—Eso no importa —dice Santa Claus. Toma la mano del Tío Pancho y—en un abrir y cerrar de ojo—bajan juntos por la chimenea, como si fuera magia.

VINCENT HURRIES DOWN the ladder and peeks through the window. His tío is already wearing his old mariachi outfit. His belly is about to split his pants wide open! The fancy coat is coming apart at the seams. Even Uncle Pancho's much-trusted guitar—la Little Lulu—is missing several of its strings.

VICENTE BAJA la escalera con prisa y se asoma por la ventana. Su tío ya tiene puesto su viejo traje de mariachi. ¡Su panza casi revienta sus pantalones! El saco lujoso se está deshaciendo. Y hasta le faltan cuerdas a la fiel guitarra del Tío Pancho, la Pequeña Lulú.

SANTA CLAUS REACHES INTO his pocket and pulls out hundreds of tiny colored stars and sprinkles them over Pancho's head. A golden glow fills the room, and then fades to reveal Tío Pancho transformed!— a gold jacket with matching sequined trousers, rattlesnake-skin boots with silver spurs, a big sombrero covered in gold sequins and blinking Christmas lights, a great big cape and a golden mask. Even la Little Lulu is not the same. She's a golden guitar with silver strings!

❖

SANTA CLAUS METE LA mano en su bolsa y saca cientos de estrellitas de colores que espolvorea sobre la cabeza de Pancho. Un resplandor dorado inunda la habitación, y luego se desvanece para mostrar ¡al Tío Pancho transformado! Una chamarra de oro con pantalones con lentejuelas, botas de piel de víbora con espuelas de plata, un gran sombrero cubierto con lentejuelas de oro y luces titilantes de Navidad, una gran capa y una máscara dorada. Hasta la Pequeña Lulú es distinta. Ahora es una guitarra de oro con cuerdas de plata.

"AND YOUR WAGON?" asks Santa Claus. "Where is it?"

The old broken-down wagon is in real bad shape. With a wave of his hands, Santa turns it into a brand new wagon, as white as the clouds.

"Say, *primo*, where are those little burros of yours?"

—¿Y TU CARRETA? — pregunta Santa Claus—. ¿Dónde está?

La vieja carreta destartalada está en malas condiciones. Pero con un pase de su mano, Santa Claus la convierte en una carreta nuevecita, tan blanca como las nubes.

—Oye, primo. ¿Y dónde están tus burros?

THE BURROS ARE EATING HAY in a warm corner of the barn. Santa Claus touches each burro's head and suddenly lucha libre masks and tiny capes appear on them.

"Rigo, Jaime, Freddie and Little Joe, from this day forth you will be known to the world as the incredible Flying Burritos!" says Santa Claus. The burros rise up into the air till their feet no longer touch the floor! Vincent can't believe his eyes.

LOS BURROS COMEN HENO en una tibia esquina del potrero. Santa Claus toca la cabeza de cada burro y de repente máscaras de luchador y pequeñas capas los cubren.

—Rigo, Jaime, Freddie y Little Joe, de ahora en adelante serán conocidos como los increíbles ¡Burritos Voladores! —dice Santa. ¡Los burros se alzan en el aire hasta que sus pies no tocan el suelo! Vicente no puede creer lo que está viendo.

"AND LAST, BUT NOT LEAST, you'll never run out of presents. See this sack filled with magic dust? When you come to a house, just reach into it and pull out the perfect gift for any boy or girl. What do you say, *primo*? Will you do it? Will you help me?"

Tío Pancho smiles at his cousin Santa Claus.

"*Seguro, primo,*" he declares proudly. "I will help you!"

—Y POR ÚLTIMO, nunca se te acabarán los regalos. ¿Ves este costal lleno de polvo mágico? Cuando llegas a una casa, metes la mano y sacas el regalo perfecto para cualquier niño o niña. ¿Qué dices, primo? ¿Me ayudas?

El Tío Pancho sonríe a su primo Santa Claus.

—Seguro, primo —dice con orgullo—. ¡Yo te ayudaré!

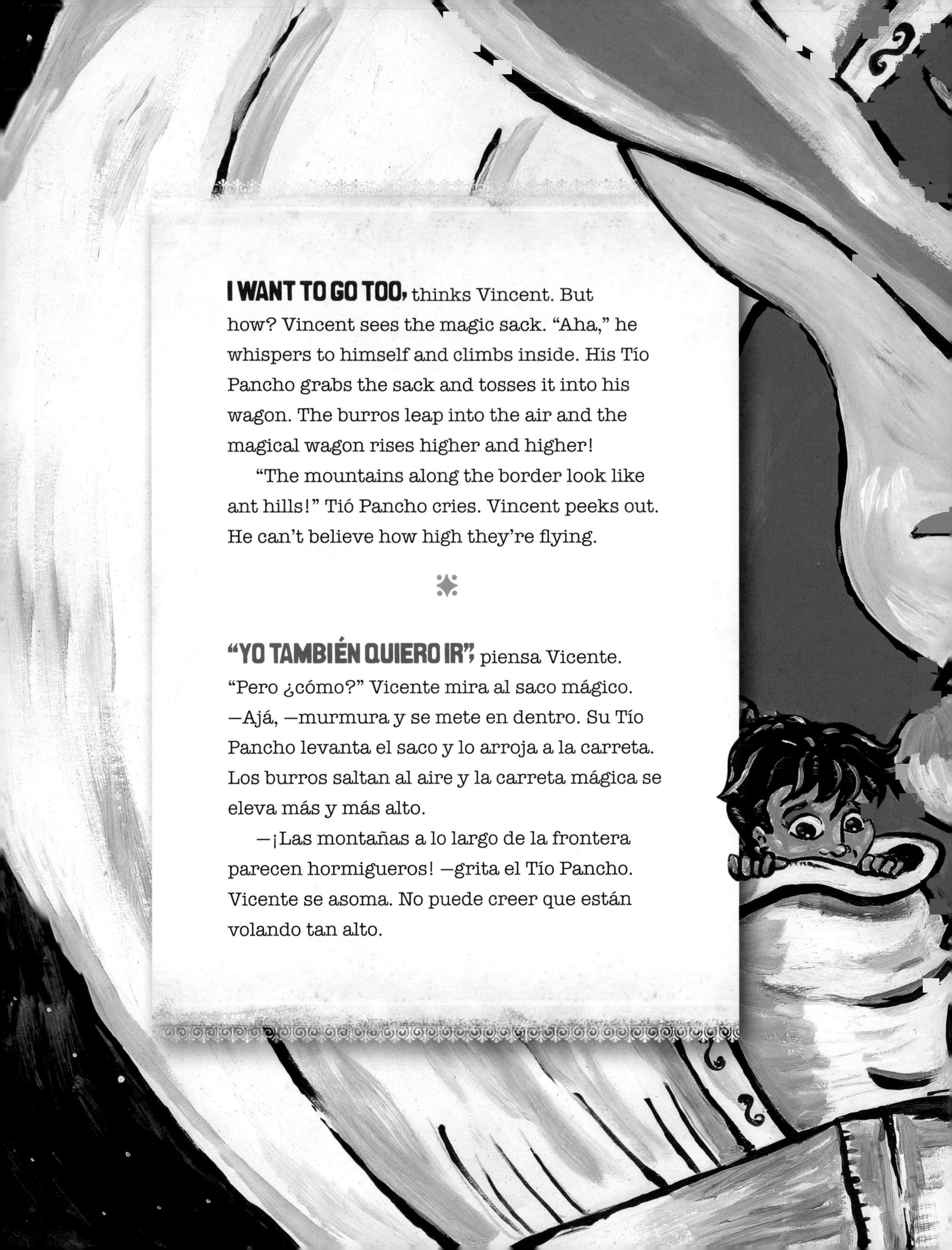

I WANT TO GO TOO, thinks Vincent. But how? Vincent sees the magic sack. "Aha," he whispers to himself and climbs inside. His Tío Pancho grabs the sack and tosses it into his wagon. The burros leap into the air and the magical wagon rises higher and higher!

"The mountains along the border look like ant hills!" Tió Pancho cries. Vincent peeks out. He can't believe how high they're flying.

"YO TAMBIÉN QUIERO IR", piensa Vicente. "Pero ¿cómo?" Vicente mira al saco mágico. —Ajá, —murmura y se mete en dentro. Su Tío Pancho levanta el saco y lo arroja a la carreta. Los burros saltan al aire y la carreta mágica se eleva más y más alto.

—¡Las montañas a lo largo de la frontera parecen hormigueros! —grita el Tío Pancho. Vicente se asoma. No puede creer que están volando tan alto.

PANCHO SOON ARRIVES at his first house. He grabs the sack and, quick as a lightning bolt, he's down the chimney and standing in front of the family's Christmas tree. He reaches into his magic bag and pulls out—his nephew Vincent!

"Nephew, what are you doing here?"

But before Vincent can answer, a voice says, "You're not Santa Claus!" Pancho and Vincent spin around to see a little girl staring at both of them.

PANCHO PRONTO LLEGA a la primera casa. Toma el costal y rápido, como un relámpago, baja por la chimenea y se para frente al árbol de Navidad de la familia. Mete la mano al costal mágico y saca a—¡su sobrino Vicente!

—Sobrino, ¿qué estás haciendo aquí?

Pero antes que Vicente responda, una voz dice: —¡Tú no eres Santa Claus!

Pancho y Vicente voltean para ver a una niñita que los está viendo.

"WELL...IT'S TRUE. I'M NOT SANTA CLAUS," whispers Pancho. "But I am his Mexican cousin. Santa Claus needed some help this year taking care of the border, you see, so he asked me for help."

"What's your name?" the little girl asks.

"My name?"

—PUES...ES VERDAD, YO NO SOY SANTA CLAUS —murmura Pancho—. Pero sí soy su primo mexicano. Santa Claus necesitó ayuda este año para encargarse de la frontera, ¿ves?, así que me pidió ayuda.

—¿Cómo te llamas?

—¿Cómo me llamo?

"HIS NAME IS CHARRO CLAUS," declares Vincent, rolling his rrrss very grandly.

"Charro Claus," says the little girl. "That's a funny name. What's a charro?"

"A charro is a Mexican cowboy who sings and plays the guitar," Vincent tells her.

"I like that. Charro Claus!" the little girl claps her hands.

❖

—SU NOMBRE ES CHARRO CLAUS— declara Vicente, pronunciando con fuerza las erres.

—Charro Claus —dice la niñita—. Es un nombre chistoso. ¿Qué es un charro?

—Un charro es un vaquero mexicano que canta y toca la guitarra —le dice Vicente.

—¡Eso me gusta, Charro Claus! —dice la niñita aplaudiendo.

CHARRO CLAUS BEGINS playing the softest-sounding lullaby he knows, with a tiny mariachi riff at the end. Soon the little girl is fast asleep on the couch. "In the morning she will think that we were just a dream," he whispers to Vincent, a big smile on his face. Vincent smiles too, and they jump up the chimney together.

CHARRO CLAUS EMPIEZA a tocar la canción de cuna más tierna que conoce, con un pequeño ritmo de mariachi al final. Pronto, la niña está bien dormida en el sillón.

—En la mañana pensará que solo fuimos un sueño —murmura a Vicente con una gran sonrisa en su cara. Vicente también sonríe, y juntos suben por la chimenea.

ON THAT CHRISTMAS EVE, Vincent helps his Tío Pancho deliver toys to all the boys and girls who live along the Texas / Mexico border. Not even rain or cloudy skies or walls or wire fences keep them from crossing back and forth to El Paso and to Ciudad Juárez, to Roma and to Miguel Alemán, to Rio Grande City and to Camargo. On that big starry night, there's no town or city, no matter how big or small, that the newly named Charro Claus forgets.

How could he? The border is his home!

TODA ESA NOCHEBUENA, Vicente ayuda a su Tío Pancho a entregar juguetes a todos los niños y niñas que viven a lo largo de la frontera Tejas y México. Ni la lluvia ni las nubes ni las paredes ni las cercas de alambre les previenen cruzar de un lado a otro, de El Paso a Ciudad Juárez, de Roma a Miguel Alemán, de Río Grande City a Camargo. En esa noche estrellada no hay un solo pueblo o ciudad, por más grande o pequeña, que se le olvida a Charro Claus.

¿Cómo podría? ¡La frontera es su hogar!

U. S. A.

MEXICO

"DID YOU LIKE HELPING ME?" Tío Pancho asks Vincent when they get home.

"I loved it," declares Vincent. "I want to help you every year!"

"Then I have just the name for you," says Tío Pancho. "The Tejas Kid!" A mask, cape, hat and guitar magically appear on his nephew Vincent. From that moment on, Tío Pancho and Vincent become known as Charro Claus and the Tejas Kid!

✦

—¿TE GUSTÓ AYUDARME? —le pregunta Tío Pancho a Vicente cuando llegan a casa.

—Me encantó —dijo Vicente—. ¡Te quiero ayudar cada año!

—Entonces ya tengo un nombre para ti —dice el Tío Pancho—. El Tejas Kid. Una máscara, capa, sombrero y guitarra aparecen mágicamente sobre su sobrino Vicente. De ese momento en adelante, Tío Pancho y Vicente se convierten en ¡Charro Claus and the Tejas Kid!

DO YOU LIVE NEAR THE BORDER between Texas and Mexico? Well, don't be surprised if you happen to look up in the sky one Christmas Eve night and see a wagon being pulled by a pack of flying burritos. If you listen closely you might even hear Charro Claus and his sidekick the Tejas Kid calling out for all the world to hear:

"*Ándale*, Rigo! Go, Jaime! C'mon, Freddie! *Dale gaaaaaas*, Little Joe! Step on it!"

Y TÚ, ¿VIVES EN LA FRONTERA, entre Tejas y México? Pues que no te sorprenda si miras hacia el cielo una Nochebuena y ves una carreta jalada por unos burritos voladores. Y si escuchas con cuidado, tal vez oigas al Charro Claus y su ayudante, el Tejas Kid, gritando para que todo el mundo los oiga:

—¡Ándale, Rigo! ¡Vamos, Jaime! ¡Síguele, Freddie! ¡Dale gaaaaaas, Little Joe!

(YES, VIRGINIA) SANTA CLAUS HAS A MEXICAN COUSIN...

Like so many kids, I didn't even know that Santa Claus had a Mexican cousin. But that changed one day when I was around four years old. I was with my father at the grocery store in my hometown in South Texas—Rio Grande City. The store was having a special promotion. For not too much money, children could have their picture taken with Santa Claus. The prospect of seeing Santa Claus *in the flesh* was really exciting to me, so I stood in line with the rest of the kids.

As I got closer to Santa, however, I noticed right away that something wasn't right. Why was Santa Claus sitting in a horse-drawn wagon instead of his magical sleigh? He was also dressed in a very strange manner, even stranger than his usual red-and-white outfit. Even though he was wearing his traditional red jacket and trousers, those trousers were tucked neatly into black cowboy boots attached to a pair of oversized silver spurs. A grand serape decorated in the colors of the Mexican flag was draped across his left shoulder, and an oversized mariachi hat rested on his head.

"Who is this man?" I wondered. He certainly didn't look like any Santa Claus that I had ever seen. I grabbed my father's hand and told him in no uncertain terms that this man was an imposter—"Dad! This is not Santa Claus!"

My father turned to me and smiled. It was then that he uttered the words that served as the inspiration for this book.

"No *mijo*, it's true. This isn't Santa Claus," he answered me, "but he *is* his Mexican cousin."

"Santa Claus has a Mexican cousin?" I asked. How could this be? How was it possible? Who was this Mexican Santa Claus? Where did he come from? Did he deliver presents to all the children of the world too?

My father left all these questions unanswered. And they stayed unanswered until the day when one of my elementary teachers played a song on the record player. It was the story of a Mexican Santa Claus!

A man named Lalo Guerrero had actually composed this song. It was called *Pancho Claus*. In a lot of ways, the song was a Mexicanized version of *The Night before Christmas*. I loved that song and sang it over and over until I knew every word.

One year I even met Pancho Claus. He delivered presents to all the kids who lived in my neighborhood. He did this by dropping tightly wrapped bundles from a low-flying airplane that zoomed over all our houses. These bundles were jam-packed with candies and toys.

Years later I found out about yet another Pancho Claus when I met actor

Richard Reyes from Houston. He was in a musical based on a Mexican Santa Claus, a zoot suit-wearing good guy who drove around in a Fiesta low-rider delivering presents to all the kids in the barrio. As Pancho Claus, Richard Reyes has done a lot of work with young kids and the community through an outreach known as the Pancho Claus Art and Education Project.

After my son Vincent was born, I wanted to share with him the wonder and pride that I had felt when I first learned that Santa Claus had a Mexican cousin. I decided to write my own version of this tale, filtered through the many stories and encounters I had had with that esteemed celebrity. And I decided to give *my* Mexican Santa his own special name: Charro Claus! I got that name from my memories of the Mexican movies that I saw as a child with my grandmother. Famed Mexican singers like Pedro Infante and Jorge Negrete would dress up as *charros*, Mexican cowboys who would sing captivating songs to beautiful women to win their hearts.

I wanted my little son Vincent to meet Charro Claus. What better way than to put him right into the story so he could become part of the mystery and lore surrounding Santa's *primo*? After much thinking and tinkering and drawing, the Tejas Kid was born. I told my wife Irma that our Vincent will have fun telling his friends that he is the boy behind the mask of the Tejas Kid.

Órale. So there you have it. These are all the things that led to the creation of the story of Charro Claus and the Tejas Kid. Why don't you come visit us down here in Texas right around Christmas time? If you do, maybe you can see Charro Claus riding alongside his cousin Santa Claus at the annual Holiday River Parade in San Antonio, or catch a glimpse of him and his magical burros flying over the roof tops of old Rio Grande City. You might even spy him and the Tejas Kid as they soar back and forth across the U.S. / Mexico border. If you do, make sure that you wave at the funny man in the large charro hat with the blinking Christmas lights. It will make him so happy.

And since you're in Texas, remember when you see him to call out,

¡FELIZ NAVIDAD!

This book is dedicated to the memory of my father, Margarito, who first introduced me to the fact that Santa Claus had a Mexican cousin; and my son, Vincent Ventura Garza, the inspiration and model for the Tejas Kid.

CHARRO CLAUS AND THE TEJAS KID. Copyright © 2008 by Xavier Garza. All rights reserved. No part of this book may be used or reproduced in any manner whatsoever without written consent from the publisher, except for brief quotations for reviews. For further information, write Cinco Puntos Press, 701 Texas Avenue, El Paso, TX 79901; or call 1-915-838-1625. Printed in Hong Kong.

FIRST EDITION
10 9 8 7 6 5 4 3 2 1

Library of Congress Cataloging-in-Publication Data

Garza, Xavier.
 Charro Claus and the Tejas Kid / written and illustrated by Xavier Garza. -- 1st ed.
    p. cm.
 Summary: One Christmas Eve, Santa Claus asks his cousin Pancho to help him deliver toys to the boys and girls along the Texas-Mexico border, and when he agrees, Santa magically transforms him into Charro Claus.
 ISBN 978-1-933693-24-8 (alk. paper)
 [1. Santa Claus--Fiction. 2. Christmas--Fiction. 3. Mexican Americans--Fiction. 4. Mexican-American Border Region--Fiction. 5. Humorous stories.] I. Title.

PZ7.G21188Ch 2008
[E]--dc22

2008011635

Translation by Luis Humberto Crosthwaite.
Cover design by Sergio Gomez. Book design by Paco Casas
Good friends of ours!

OTHER GREAT BILINGUAL BOOKS FROM CINCO PUNTOS PRESS

✦

Lucha Libre: The Man in the Silver Mask
Written and illustrated by Xavier Garza

Ghost Fever / Mal de Fantasma
By Joe Hayes. Illustrated by Mona Pennypacker

La Llorona / The Weeping Woman
As told by Joe Hayes. Illustrated by Vicki Trego Hill

The Day it Snowed Tortillas / El Dia Que Nevaron Tortillas
By Joe Hayes. Illustrated by Antonio Castro L

El Cucuy!: A Bogeyman Cuento in English and Spanish
As told by Joe Hayes. Illustrated by Honorio Robledo

Dance, Nana, Dance / Baila, Nana, Baila
By Joe Hayes. Illustrated by Mauricio Trenard Sayago

¡Sí Se Puede! / Yes, We Can!
By Diana Cohn. Illustrated by Francisco Delgado

A Gift from Papá Diego / Un Regalo de Papá Diego
By Benjamin Alire Sáenz. Illustrated by Geronimo Garcia

A Perfect Season for Dreaming / Un Tiempo Perfecto Para Soñar
By Benjamín Alire Sáenz. Illustrated by Esau Andrade Valencia

✦

www.cincopuntos.com